SUPER STAR PROBLEMS

Also by Heather Grovet

Ready to Ride series
A Perfect Star
Zippitty Do Dah
Good As Gold
Blondie's Big Ride
A Friend for Zipper

Other books by Heather Grovet
Beanie: The Horse That Wasn't a Horse
Marvelous Mark and His No-good Dog
Petunia, the Ugly Pug
Prince: The Persnickety Pony That Didn't Like Grown-ups
Prince Prances Again
Sarah Lee and a Mule Named Maybe
What's Wrong With Rusty?

SUPER STAR PROBLEMS

Heather Grovet *Series Book Six*

READY TO RIDE SERIES

Pacific Press® Publishing Association
Nampa, Idaho
Oshawa, Ontario, Canada
www.pacificpress.com

Book design by Gerald Lee Monks
Cover illustration © Mary Bausman
Inside design by Aaron Troia

Additional copies of this book are available
by calling toll-free 1-800-765-6955 or
by visiting http://www.adventistbookcenter.com.

Library of Congress Cataloging-in-Publication Data

Grovet, Heather, 1963-
Super Star problems / Heather Grovet.
p. cm.—(Ready to ride; bk. 6)
Summary: Trusting in God, ten-year-old Kendra tries to repair her
friendship with another rider in the Ready to Ride pony club.
ISBN 13: 978-0-8163-2255-8 (pbk.)
ISBN 10: 0-8163-2255-4 (pbk.)
[1. Ponies—Fiction. 2. Clubs—Fiction. 3. Friendship—Fiction. 4.
Conduct of life—Fiction. 5. Christian life—Fiction.] I. Title.
PZ7.G931825Su 2008
[Fic]—dc22

2008021765

08 09 10 11 12 • 5 4 3 2 1

Dedication

To my daughter, Danelle Grovet. Thanks for the crazy tiger and pony ideas!

Contents

Ready to Pole Bend

Three girls sat on their ponies in the center of the Rawlings' large riding pen. They were Kendra Rawling on her white Welsh pony, Star; Megan Lewis and her Palomino pony, Blondie; and Ruth-Ann Chow with her little Paint horse, Zipper.

"Megan, do you remember how to make your new watch work like a stopwatch?" Kendra asked. She reached over to pat Star's silky neck.

Megan looked puzzled. "I think so," she said. "Why?"

"I want to show you how fast Star can run the pole-bending pattern before we quit," Kendra said. "And I want you to time us."

"I'm going to put Zipper away," Ruth-Ann said, dismounting from the Paint. "I don't want him to be tired at tomorrow's gymkhana."

"Zipper didn't work very hard today," Kendra said. "We've only been out here for half an hour or so."

"It's hard work trotting," Ruth-Ann said with a grin.

"I would think that making Zipper trot in this heat was hard work for *you*," Megan said. "But it probably wasn't too tiring for Zipper."

"Maybe not," Ruth-Ann agreed. "But I still think we should quit for today."

"OK," Kendra said. "But wait a minute until I've run Star through the pattern." She looked at the row of poles that stood in a line at the far side of the arena. Star raised her head and looked at the poles too, as if she were also thinking about the pattern.

"I'm ready any time you are," Megan said, rolling back her sleeve so her watch was exposed.

"I don't think you should run Star," Ruth-Ann said. "One of you could get hurt."

"Uh-oh," Megan said. "Who's being a worrywart today?"

"I'm not a wart," Ruth-Ann said. "Warts are all lumpy and gross! I just don't want anyone to get hurt."

"How could running the pole-bending pattern hurt Star or me?" Kendra asked.

"You could fall off and land on your head!" Ruth-Ann said.

"Maybe," Kendra said. "But I don't fall off very often. And I'm wearing my helmet."

"And Kendra has a hard head, anyhow!" Megan said, laughing. "Star isn't very tall, so she'd probably survive."

"Well, maybe Star would trip and hurt her leg," Ruth-Ann suggested.

"Would that make her a falling Star?" Megan asked.

"Ha-ha," Ruth-Ann said.

"Star isn't going to fall," Kendra insisted. "She's very careful."

"What else could happen?" Megan asked, turning to Ruth-Ann.

"Star could learn bad habits," Ruth-Ann said. "Trish told us that ponies who are raced a lot think they should run all the time."

"Do you think Zipper would want to run all the time?" Megan asked.

"Not a chance!" Ruth-Ann said.

"Blondie might," Megan said. "It's easy to get her excited. That's why I'm not going to run her tomorrow."

"You know I don't run Star very often," Kendra said. "In fact, I've never even galloped her through the pole-bending pattern. But if we're supposed to race tomorrow at the gymkhana, then we should try it at least once when we're at home. Right?"

Ruth-Ann's face broke into a smile. "OK," she said. "If you aren't going to fall off and hurt your head, break Star's leg, or develop bad habits, then you'd better get out there and run!"

"Are you finished worrying?" Megan asked.

"Oh, I wasn't worried," Ruth-Ann said.

"You sounded worried to me," Megan said.

"Nope, I just didn't want Zipper's feelings to be hurt."

"Now I'm really confused," Kendra said. "Why would Zipper's feelings be hurt if Star and I run the pole-bending pattern?"

"Zipper would be depressed because he can't run nearly as fast as the girl horses!" Ruth-Ann said. She looked down at her Paint horse, which stood with his eyes half closed in the sunlight.

The girls laughed.

The three of us will always be friends, Kendra thought happily.

The previous year the girls had started a club called Ready to Ride. The trio spent hours together with their ponies. Sometimes they went for long trail rides through the pasture; at other times they practiced riding in the Lewises' arena. Best of all, they had starting taking riding lessons from a wonderful woman named Trish Klein.

The next day would be July 1, which was Canada Day. The town of Alliance was having a special sports day celebration with a parade, baseball games, and a gymkhana open to adults and kids of all ages. The girls and their ponies had been practicing for weeks, and they were looking forward to seeing how they would do in the competition.

Kendra reached down to check Star's cinch. It was a bit loose, so she slid out of the saddle and tightened it a notch. Star nuzzled Kendra's hand, making the girl smile.

Star was the most beautiful pony a girl could ever want! She was a dainty snow-white Welsh pony with a beautiful dished face and tiny pointed ears. Everything about her was as pretty as a pony could be. And Star seemed to enjoy the racing games almost as much as Kendra did.

"Is your helmet on tight enough?" Megan asked.

Kendra rolled her eyes. "Now I suppose it's your turn to start worrying!" she said.

"Nope," Megan said. "But friends sometimes have to remind other friends to be careful."

"You're right," Kendra said. She unsnapped her bright pink riding helmet and pushed her long brown hair off her face. Then Kendra slid the helmet back into place and adjusted the harness tight under her chin. "There," she said. "Now both Star and I are snugged up and ready to go!"

"Trish said I don't have to make Zipper run to-morrow," Ruth-Ann said. "She said we won't be good at the races, but we could do well in some of the other games, even if we don't rush."

"Trish knows Zipper won't gallop anyhow!" Megan joked. "He likes to save his energy for more important things."

"He saves his energy for eating," Ruth-Ann said, chuckling.

"Especially if it's eating licorice or other candies," Kendra said. Zipper nodded his head, making his two-toned brown-and-white mane flap up and down. He seemed to be saying *Candy! Yum, yum!*

"I think Zipper understood every word we said," Megan said.

"Trish said that sometimes Zipper is too smart for his own good," Ruth-Ann agreed.

"Blondie's smart too," Megan said.

Trish had taught the girls how to jump their ponies and helped them prepare for their very first horse show the previous summer. She had helped them solve problems such as slowing energetic Blondie down and speeding lazy Zipper up! For the last month they had been working on the barrel racing and pole-bending patterns for the Canada Day gymkhana.

Kendra swung back into the saddle and moved the white pony forward. "I think we're ready to go," she said. "Have you figured out how the stopwatch works, Megan? I'd like to know how fast we are."

"I think so," Megan replied. She pushed buttons on the watch for a moment and then nodded her head. "OK."

"Ladies and gentlemen," Ruth-Ann said in a loud voice, "please put your hands together to welcome our next contestant—Kendra Rawling and her pony, A Perfect Star."

"Hurrah!" Megan said. Megan and Ruth-Ann clapped their hands.

"Quit clapping and tell me when to go," Kendra said with a giggle.

"Are you ready?" Megan asked.

Kendra nodded.

"On your mark, get set, go!"

Kendra leaned forward and squeezed her legs. Star trotted a step or two and then lifted off into a canter.

Kendra had run the pole-bending pattern so many times, she felt she could do it in her sleep. But as she pushed Star's easy canter into a brisk gallop, suddenly everything seemed to pass in a blur.

They rushed past the row of poles and at the very end, spun a sharp left. Kendra reined the little mare back and forth through the poles in a zigzag pattern, being careful not to knock anything down.

At the end of the line, they slowed briefly and then twirled right, ran through the poles again, and then spun around and raced toward the finish line.

"Go! Go! Go!" Ruth-Ann and Megan cheered together.

Kendra squeezed her legs harder, and Star shot across the finish line.

"Twenty-four seconds," Megan shouted. "That was awesome!"

"You're going to outrun everyone," Ruth-Ann said. "Even the grown-ups!"

"Your pony's a superstar," Megan added.

"Super Star!" Both girls clapped their hands as Star and Kendra walked back across the ring toward them. Star seemed pleased and tossed her head proudly.

From across the riding ring another person clapped his hands. The girls looked up in surprise. A slim boy about their age, with reddish brown hair and freckles, stood outside the riding ring. He saw the R2R Club members looking at him and raised his hand to wave.

Kendra's New Neighbors

"Who's that?" Ruth-Ann asked. The boy waved again and then slid through the rails of the fence and began to walk in their direction.

"That's Matt, I think," Kendra said.

"You think?"

"His family bought Mr. Granger's house," Kendra said. "They have four kids, and they're all boys."

"Four boys? Yuck!" Megan said.

"I have two brothers and that's more than enough!" Ruth-Ann groaned.

"These boys all look nearly the same," Kendra said. "Except some are bigger than others."

The boy stopped and reached over to pat Star's nose. "Your horse can run pretty fast," he said.

"Star isn't a horse," Kendra said. "She's a pony."

"Do you like ponies?" Ruth-Ann asked.

"I don't know," the boy said with a shrug. "I've never had one. In fact, we've never had any pets, not even a dog or cat." He patted Star's nose again. A bit too firmly, Kendra thought. Star snorted and raised her head.

"Are you Matt?" Megan asked. "Or one of the other boys?"

"I'm Matthew Ryan Van Dresser," the boy said. "But everyone calls me Matt. I'm almost twelve years old."

"What are your brothers' names?" Ruth-Ann asked.

"Jessie is my big brother; he's fourteen," Matt said. "Daniel is ten and Todd is nine. So I'm the middle one."

"Is it fun having that many brothers?" Ruth-Ann asked.

"Brothers are OK, I guess," Matt said. "At least most of the time."

"Ruth-Ann has an older brother, Max, who's about your age," Kendra said. "And she has a little brother and sister too."

"Do you like living here?" Megan asked.

"I like living in the country," Matt replied. "No one complains if we make a lot of noise."

"You have enough space to keep a pony or two,"

Kendra suggested. "Would you like a pony of your own?"

"Not really," Matt said.

The three girls looked at each other. *Not want a pony?*

"What will you do with all that grass if you don't have a pony?" Megan asked.

"Dad says he's going to buy some sheep to keep the grass down," the boy said. "No one wants to mow all that lawn." He reached over and rubbed Blondie briskly on the forehead.

"Ponies are better than sheep," Ruth-Ann said. "You can ride a pony."

"I rode a sheep once," Matt said. "At a Little Buckaroo Rodeo. I even won a prize for staying on the longest."

"Are you coming to the Alliance Sports Day?" Kendra asked. "There won't be a rodeo, but there will be ball games and some pony races."

"I might come," Matt responded. "I'm not sure."

"I think ponies would be better to ride than sheep," Megan said.

"Probably," Matt said. He reached over to pet Zipper this time. "I like the color of your horse," he told Ruth-Ann. "He's kind of a neat color, almost brown and almost red."

"He's a sorrel," Ruth-Ann said.

"His hair's exactly the same color as yours," Megan said.

"Does that mean I'm a sorrel?" Matt asked. "When I was little I always wanted to be a horse." He neighed.

The girls laughed.

"A pony would keep the grass as short as sheep would," Kendra said. "And Star would like to have another horse nearby to keep her company. Zipper and Blondie don't live here; they just come to visit sometimes."

"It did look like racing around on a pony would be fun," Matt said. "Almost as much fun as racing my dirt bike."

"You can't run a pony very often," Megan said. "Or else they'll get hyper and stop listening to you."

"Then a motorcycle is probably better," Matt said. "I can go as fast as I want, and my motorcycle doesn't ever disobey."

"I don't think Star's ever seen a motorcycle," Kendra said. "Is your bike really big?"

"Is it really noisy?" Megan asked.

"Will it scare our ponies?" Ruth-Ann wondered.

"Why would a motorcycle scare a pony?" Matt asked. "I'm not going to run into them with it."

"They wouldn't know that at first," Kendra said.

"Ponies aren't very brave."

"Hmm," Matt said. "I didn't know that either. In fact, I don't know very much about ponies at all."

He reached up and began to pet Zipper's brown ears. Zipper shook his head.

"I'll teach you something about ponies," Ruth-Ann said.

"What?" Matt asked.

"They don't like to have their ears rubbed very much," Ruth-Ann said. "See, look at Zipper's face. He doesn't look very happy when you're doing that."

"Oh," Matt said. He stopped rubbing.

"And ponies like you to pet their faces very gently," Kendra said. "Otherwise it hurts."

"Motorcycles are better," Matt decided. "A bike never complains about anything. You can drop it or kick it and it doesn't care."

"Motorcycles are boring compared to ponies," Kendra said.

"Not to me," Matt said.

The R2R Club looked at each other and frowned. *How could anyone think a motorcycle was better than a horse?*

"Do your brothers all have motorcycles too?" Megan asked.

"Just Jessie and I have motorcycles right now,"

Matt said. "But soon I'm going to sell mine to Daniel. I'm getting too big for it, and I need a new one." He looked at Kendra and Star. "Your pony isn't very big either. Maybe you need to sell it and buy a new one too."

"Star is just the right size for me," Kendra said indignantly.

"In a few years your feet are going to drag on the ground," Matt continued.

"Star fits me perfectly," Kendra said. "And when I get too big to ride her, I'm going to buy a pony cart. Then I can use her forever and ever."

"A pony cart would seem slow compared to my motorcycle," Matt said.

"But a pony's a lot more fun than a machine," Kendra said. "Ponies can be your friends."

"Supper time!" A faint shout came from across the yard.

Matt grinned. "That's my mom," he said. "I'm starving." He turned to go and then stopped. "Tomorrow I'll ride my motorcycle and show it to you."

"We won't be home tomorrow," Kendra said. "We're going to the Alliance gymkhana."

Matt didn't seem to hear them. He was already jogging across the riding ring and in a few moments disappeared from sight in the trees that separated the two homes.

"Boys!" Megan sighed.

"Boys are awful," Ruth-Ann agreed. "I feel sorry for you, Kendra, with four boys for neighbors. Think of all the problems they're going to cause."

"They haven't been too bad yet," Kendra said. "But one of them must own a drum set. I hear them play it for hours on end."

"You're going to need earplugs for Star," Megan said.

"Star ignored the drums," Kendra said. "She doesn't get frightened by very many things." Kendra slid off Star's back and loosened the pony's cinch. "I think Star's had enough work for the day. I don't want her to be too tired for tomorrow's races."

"If Star runs the pole-bending pattern like that tomorrow, you're sure to win a prize," Megan said.

"And we're doing really well on our barrel racing too," Kendra said. "I think we're going to have a really good day at the gymkhana races."

"I'm looking forward to the sack race," Ruth-Ann said eagerly. "As long as Zipper doesn't think I'm in a bag of grain and try to eat me!"

Trish had spent some time explaining the various gymkhana games to the girls. Among the timed races were the barrel race, the pole-bending race, and the keyhole race. Then there would be many different games to play that involved good riding skills and a brave pony, rather than great speed.

In the sack race, each rider had to jump with both feet in a burlap bag while they led their pony beside them. In the egg race, the rider had to balance an egg on a spoon while riding their horse across the ring.

"The boot race sounds like the most fun to me!" Megan said. In the boot race, all the competitors had to take off their riding boots and place them at the far end of the ring in a big heap. At a signal from the judge, they were to rush their ponies to the stack of footwear, find their boots and get them on, and then lead the ponies back across the line as fast as they could go.

The girls agreed that while each of the ponies had special talents, Star was the one that seemed most likely to win any of the gymkhana races. She was small and quick. She didn't insist on going slow all the time, as Zipper did. And she didn't get frazzled and flustered in a crowd the way Blondie would.

As Kendra slid her saddle off Star's back, she couldn't help smiling to herself. The next day would be so much fun. Maybe she'd even come home with a handful of ribbons to hang on her wall with the horse show ribbons she had earned the previous summer.

Kendra had been praying about the gymkhana for weeks. She had tried not to pray for ribbons and prizes, but sometimes it was difficult! Being a good sport was more important. Being fair and honest and hardworking was important too. But Kendra had to admit to herself that winning prizes sometimes seemed pretty important as well.

I'm sure God knows how hard I've worked, Kendra thought. She picked up a blue plastic currycomb and began to brush Star's sweaty back. Star shifted her feet and sighed contentedly.

Kendra loved the rich salty smell of the ponies. She loved the feel of their velvety muzzles and sleek summer coats. She loved the rhythmic sound of their hooves clip-clopping across the ground. And most of all, she loved the way ponies looked.

Zipper and Blondie were cute ponies, but deep down in her heart Kendra knew that they weren't nearly as beautiful as Star. There was something so special about the white pony that often made Kendra stop and stare. Maybe it was Star's face—her big brown eyes framed with long dark lashes, and her delicate dished face that looked almost like an Arabian. Or maybe it was her thick mane that fell like a silky curtain on her neck.

And Star wasn't just a pretty pony. She was a sweet, kind, and gentle pony. Best of all, she belonged to Kendra!

The three girls were picking out their ponies' hooves when Mr. Rawling walked up to the hitching post. "Well," he said, rumpling Kendra's long hair, "how are the Ready Three Ride girls doing today?"

"What did you call us?" Kendra asked.

"Ready Three Ride," Mr. Rawling said. His face looked serious.

Ruth-Ann, Kendra, and Megan looked at each other. Mr. Rawling was famous for his jokes, but this time they weren't certain what he was talking about.

"Well," Mr. Rawling continued, "I've been thinking about your club. How can you call yourself the Ready *to* Ride Club when there are more than two of you? So I decided you must be the Ready Three Ride Club!"

"Daddy!" Kendra reached out to tickle her father in the ribs, but he quickly stepped backwards.

"And while all you girls are here, I want to remind you that I'm driving you and your ponies to the Canada Day gymkhana tomorrow. Right?"

Megan said, "My mom and dad told me to thank you for letting the ponies stay here tonight.

"And then driving us to the sports day in the morning," she added as an afterthought.

"Thanks from my family too, Mr. Rawling," Ruth-Ann said quickly.

"No problem," Mr. Rawling said. "But I just want to remind you to bring lots of money with you tomorrow."

"I've already paid my entry fees," Megan said.

"And my mom's packing me a bag lunch because we won't have time to go to the Burger Bar to eat," Ruth-Ann said.

"So what will we need the money for?" Kendra asked.

"To pay me, of course," Mr. Rawling said. "Everyone knows that it costs a lot of money to take a ride in a taxi. And I decided that if I'm going to be a Ready Three Ride pony taxi, I should be paid properly."

"How much money will we need?" Kendra asked.

"Not that much," Mr. Rawling said.

"How much?"

"Oh, about a hundred dollars," Mr. Rawling said.

"A hundred dollars!" Kendra said. "For the three of us?"

"No," Mr. Rawling said. "A hundred dollars for each of you."

"A hundred dollars for each pony?" Ruth-Ann gasped. "Isn't that a bit expensive?"

"Oh, no," Mr. Rawling said. "I'm taking the ponies for free. It's a hundred dollars per girl."

"Daddy!"

"Ponies are easy," Mr. Rawling said. "They get into

the back of the horse trailer, and they ride nice and quietly. But girls—wow—are they different!"

"What sort of things do girls do, Mr. Rawling?" Megan asked.

"They leave makeup and curling irons in my truck," Mr. Rawling said.

"We don't curl our hair," Megan said.

"And makeup is gross," Ruth-Ann said.

"Well." Mr. Rawling thought for a moment. "Girls stare out the windows and whistle at all the boys."

"Daddy, we don't even like boys!" Kendra said.

"And I don't even know how to whistle," Megan said.

"Boys are even grosser than makeup," Ruth-Ann added.

"Now I know you girls are pulling my leg," Mr. Rawling said. "I saw the three of you talking to a boy a few minutes ago. Next thing I know, one of you will be married to him!"

"Yuck!" the girls all exclaimed together.

"The only boy I like is Zipper," Ruth-Ann said. She threw her arms around her little Paint horse's neck and gave him a squeeze.

Mr. Rawling made a sad face. The R2R girls looked at him. "Oh," Ruth-Ann said quickly. "I like you too, Mr. Rawling."

"Me too, Daddy," Kendra said.

"Me three," Megan agreed.

"Do you girls always agree on everything?" Mr. Rawling asked.

"You bet," Kendra said. "We're best friends, and best friends never disagree."

"I'm not so sure about that," Mr. Rawling said with a sigh. "But I guess I'll let you girls ride in my truck for free this time. But remember, I don't want any curling irons burning a hole in my seat covers. OK?"

"OK," Megan said.

"We promise, Daddy," Kendra said.

"Oh, and I'm supposed to give you a message, Megan," Mr. Rawling said. "Your mom says supper's ready."

"Great!" Megan said. "We're having lasagna tonight."

"Lucky you!" Kendra said. "Maybe I should see if I can eat at your house too."

"Hey!" Mr. Rawling said. "I'm cooking tonight, so the food will be great."

"Tomato soup?" Kendra guessed.

"Nope," Mr. Rawling said.

"That's all you cook," Kendra said.

"Not true," Mr. Rawling said. He hesitated for a moment and then grinned at the R2R girls. "I warm up great mushroom soup too."

With a groan, the girls led their ponies to the small wooden corral and locked them inside. Kendra threw a few flakes of hay over the fence.

"Good night, Super Star," she called as she dusted bits of alfalfa off her pants. "Sleep well. We'll have a busy day tomorrow."

That night the ponies would have a sleepover together so they would be close by for Mr. Rawling to take them to the gymkhana. The Alliance Sports Day was going to be so much fun!

Kendra had worked very hard to teach Star the barrel racing and pole-bending patterns. Soon she would see how she compared to all the other children her age. She would get to spend the day with her wonderful pony and her two best friends. And maybe, just maybe, she would win a bunch of ribbons to make the great day even better!

Fireworks!

After supper Kendra cleared the soup dishes off the table. Then she hurried around the kitchen, packing lunch for the gymkhana the next day. She made a cheese-and-tomato sandwich, and also packed an orange, two cookies, a juice box, and a zipper bag of mixed nuts.

"You might want to freeze some water in your water bottle," Mrs. Rawling suggested. "It's supposed to get hot tomorrow."

That sounded like a good idea to Kendra, so she filled her plastic bottle half full of water and slipped it into the freezer. Then she headed to her room to make certain she had her best riding clothes set aside for the big day.

It was dark when Kendra finally finished all her

packing. "I thought you'd be in bed by now," Mrs. Rawling called through the open bedroom door. "You know you'll have to leave by seven in the morning tomorrow."

Seven! That was so early in the morning.

Kendra was in the bathroom brushing her teeth when she heard her father call loudly from another part of the house. "Pardon me?" Kendra called back.

"Fireworks!" Mr. Rawling shouted. "Come and see the fireworks!"

Kendra tossed her toothbrush down on the sink and rushed into the front room. The sky was lit up with a brilliant pink color. Then there was a loud *bang!* and a shot of green flew directly over their house and joined the fading pink.

"Wow!" Mr. Rawling said. "That's the closest I've ever seen fireworks before!"

"They're shooting them right over our place," Mrs. Rawling agreed. "Our new neighbors must be celebrating Canada Day a day early!"

"And they must have spent a lot of money on those fireworks," Mr. Rawling said. "Look at the size of that one!"

Another loud *thud* filled the house, followed almost immediately by a sharp string of *pop, pop, pop!*

"Those must be firecrackers," Mr. Rawling said. "They'll be low, so we can't see them."

In a moment a burst of orange and pink lit up the sky directly above the Rawlings' yard. Kendra took her eyes off the explosions for a moment and suddenly saw a strange sight.

The three ponies were visible in the glow from the fireworks, and they were racing around the corral wildly. They weren't cantering or even galloping. Instead, they were running as hard as they could, terrified by the loud noise and bright lights of the fireworks.

"Star!" For a moment Kendra had forgotten all about the ponies!

"Kendra, wait!" Mrs. Rawling called.

Without taking time to think, Kendra flung open the door and rushed down the front steps. Why hadn't she done something as soon as the fireworks had started? Kendra was almost to the corral when a burst of light and a sudden *kaboom!* lit up the yard.

Star lunged forward. Kendra saw the white mare smash into the tall wooden fence with her shoulder. She heard the crack of wood breaking.

Then it was dark. The fireworks were over as quickly as they had started.

Kendra's mother and father rushed outdoors with a flashlight. They found the three ponies still inside the corral, trembling. The dim beam from the flashlight showed the damage. Two boards on the corral were splintered.

Kendra glimpsed a scrape on Blondie's amber face. Zipper seemed OK. But Star's normally pure white coat now had a streak of bright red blood.

Kendra clambered inside the corral. The ponies were so frightened that they spooked as she came near and galloped with loud snorts to the far side of the little paddock.

"Kendra!" Mrs. Rawling called. "Come back!"

Mr. Rawling held up his hand. "Give them a minute to calm down," he said. He turned and forked some hay over the fence. The ponies continued to dash back and forth, with Blondie leading the way.

"Star!" Kendra called. The white mare paused for an instant, and then she galloped after the other ponies. Her head was raised high, and there was a wild expression in her eyes.

Finally, Zipper stopped for a moment. He looked at the pile of hay and began to move on. Then he stopped again. The sight of food was more than Zipper could resist. With a snort he lowered his head and began to eat.

Blondie and Star charged around the corral one more time and then slowed to a trot. They looked at Zipper, and they looked at the hay. Star and Blondie hesitated. They moved closer to Zipper and finally decided it was safe for them to eat also.

Kendra waited a few more moments and then

slowly stepped toward the ponies. She slipped a halter over Star's head and crooned gently to her. The little mare trembled but didn't move as Kendra ran her hand down her neck.

"You shouldn't have gone into the corral when they were running like that," Mr. Rawling said.

"You scared me half to death, Kendra," her mother agreed. "I'm not ashamed to admit that I was praying as the ponies ran past you."

"Star would never hurt me," Kendra said.

"Star would never purposely hurt you," Mrs. Rawling said. "But she was so terrified, she wasn't thinking."

"Where is she hurt?" Mr. Rawling asked.

Kendra examined the white mare's near side. It looked clean. Then she walked around the pony and looked at her right side. An enormous gaping wound sprawled across the pony's shoulder. "Oh, no!" Kendra gasped. She led Star forward.

Mr. Rawling shook his head when he saw the pony's side. "That's got to hurt," he said.

"I wonder if it will need stitches," Mrs. Rawling said with a sigh. "We better take her to the vet clinic."

"At this time of the night?" Mr. Rawling asked.

"They'll have a veterinarian on call," Mrs. Rawling said. "But we should phone ahead. Tomorrow's a holiday, so we need to make sure someone's around."

"Do you think Star's going to be OK?" Kendra asked. She blinked hard.

"Kendra." Mrs. Rawling turned to her daughter. "Star's hardly limping, so it might not be as serious as it looks. But I'm not a vet, so we should get it checked properly."

"We should pray about it too," Mr. Rawling said. For once the man wasn't joking. "God cares about Star. He'll help the vets know what to do to help her."

Kendra couldn't bring herself to look at Star's shoulder again. The red blood against her pony's white coat was just too awful.

"Let's pray right now," Mr. Rawling said. "It's fortunate that I have the truck and trailer all hooked up for tomorrow's sports day."

Sports day! The gymkhana! In all the excitement, Kendra had forgotten about their plans for the next day.

She felt a bit better as the family clasped hands and said a prayer for her pony. "Father, please help Star to be brave," Mr. Rawling prayed. "Help her feel better. Help the vet know what to do so she won't be lame."

When he was finished, Mr. Rawling opened the corral gate, and Kendra led the pony across the grass to the trailer. Kendra was worried that Star wouldn't get into the trailer without the other ponies for company, but the little mare didn't hesitate. She neatly stepped into the trailer and stood quietly while Mrs. Rawling closed the trailer door.

In a moment, they were driving down the road toward the vet clinic.

A Trip to the Vet Clinic

"Horses!" Dr. Scott said, shaking his head. "They always seem to pick the worst possible time to hurt themselves."

He bent over the pony, studying her carefully. When Dr. Scott straightened up, he pointed to the large wound on Star's shoulder. "I want to show you something, young lady," he said.

Kendra shook her head. "I can't look, Dr. Scott," she said. "Star's wound is totally disgusting."

"I thought you planned to be a veterinarian when you grew up," the man said kindly.

"I thought I did too," Kendra said. "But I feel sick when I even look at Star's chest. How could I ever be a vet?"

"You love Star," Dr. Scott said. "So that makes it different."

"Maybe."

"When my old dog was hurt last fall, I had to get another vet to do his surgery," Dr. Scott said. "Even experienced veterinarians like me have a difficult time taking care of their own animals."

"I suppose you're right," Kendra said.

"I just wanted to show you a lump that's underneath Star's skin here," Dr. Scott continued. "I think it's possible that she has a large splinter of wood embedded in her shoulder. I need to open up that area and see what's in there."

"Open it up?" Kendra asked. "Do you mean you'd have to operate?"

"Well, I won't have to give her anesthetic," Dr. Scott said. "I'll just give her a shot of medication to sedate her. She'd still be standing up, but she wouldn't have any pain. Then I can check her shoulder properly. Would that be OK with you?"

Kendra nodded slowly. "I guess so," she said.

Dr. Scott looked at Kendra's parents. They both nodded their heads. "Do whatever's necessary," Mrs. Rawling said.

"Star won't like the shot very much," Dr. Scott said. "But after that, she'll feel a lot better."

Kendra watched the veterinarian draw medication up into a syringe. She turned her head away as he injected it into the big vein in Star's neck.

SUPER STAR PROBLEMS

The pony jerked with the poke of the needle, but in a moment she began to relax. Soon she stood quietly with her head drooped and her eyes half closed.

"OK, now," Dr. Scott said. "Let's see what we've got here." He picked up several silver tools and moved toward the little mare.

Mrs. Rawling held Star's lead rope while Kendra studied the bulletin board across the room. "German Shepherd puppies for sale," a sign read. Kendra read every note on the board, keeping her eyes as far away from Star's shoulder as possible.

Before long, Dr. Scott began to hum to himself. He poked and prodded and cleaned for a few minutes. Finally, he straightened up with a smile. "There," he said. "Your pony's going to be totally fine."

"Did she need stitches?" Kendra asked.

Dr. Scott shook his head. "No," he said. "The wound's too deep to be stitched, so it will need to heal from the inside out. But look at the big piece of wood I took out of her neck." He held up something brown in the palm of his hand. Kendra quickly turned away. "Now I'll give you instructions on how to care for her, and then you'll be free to go. Her sedation will wear off before long."

Dr. Scott gave Mr. Rawling a bag full of medication and explained how it should be given to Star. The mare would need to be kept in a small pen for the next few weeks to help the wound heal. "We don't want her walking too much for a while," Dr. Scott said. "Or she could develop proud flesh." He explained that proud flesh was a type of scar that grew lumpy and could cause the pony to have problems in the future. "The best way to avoid proud flesh is to keep the wound fairly still," he said.

Then he explained that the cut would need to be cleaned with fresh water every day. One container in the bag was special ointment for the wound; another bottle contained spray that would keep flies off the sore until it healed.

"She'll be as good as new in no time at all," Dr. Scott said.

"How long will it take to heal?" Mrs. Rawling asked.

"Shoulder wounds normally heal very well," Dr. Scott replied. "A horse's shoulder has much better circulation than their leg, and therefore will repair quite quickly. So, Kendra, your pony picked a good location to be injured—if she had to be injured!"

"Will Kendra be able to ride later this summer?" Mr. Rawling asked.

"Definitely," Dr. Scott said. "Star needs two weeks of stall rest so the injury heals properly. Then she can go into a larger pen and move around slowly for about a week. After that, Kendra could start lightly riding her."

Kendra counted in her head. It would be three weeks before she could ride Star again. Three weeks was a long time without a pony. Summer would be halfway through by then!

Dr. Scott turned to look at Kendra. "But no racing around for a while, young lady," he said. "Star will need to get back into shape after her time off."

Racing!

In all the excitement of the evening, Kendra had almost forgotten about the Alliance Sports Day races. She had worked very hard to teach Star the race patterns. The little pony was fit and ready to go. She was the Ready to Ride Club's little Super Star.

And now they would miss everything.

The Rawlings would have to wait for the pony's sedation to wear off. Then it would be safe to walk Star back to the trailer. Kendra was sad and mad and close to tears as she waited. The next day Megan and Ruth-Ann would be able to ride their ponies at the sports day. Star wouldn't be going. Instead, she'd be locked in a small pen, all alone. And she'd have to stay in that pen for fourteen days!

Star would be sad to see her friends drive away. She'd want to go with them. After all, the Ready to Ride Club always did things together.

But this summer, Kendra and Star were going to miss everything.

It seemed like just a few hours since Kendra had prayed that God would help her to do her best at the sports day. That prayer wasn't going to be answered the way she had hoped.

Kendra's Sabbath School class had been studying the Lord's Prayer. Kendra could hear the words in her head. *"Thy will be done."* Was it God's will that Star get hurt? Was it God's choice that Star would have to spend weeks locked in a little pen and that her owner couldn't ride?

Dr. Scott had said Star was going to be healthy and strong again. But it would take a long time. Three weeks meant that Kendra wouldn't be able to ride until almost August!

No, this wasn't God's fault, Kendra decided. God didn't ever want bad things to happen. But this was someone's fault.

The new neighbors had made a terrible mistake. They had shot fireworks straight over the Rawlings' house. They hadn't considered warning the family so the three ponies could be put somewhere safe. They didn't know anything about horses.

It had been a dangerous and foolish thing to do, and no doubt they didn't know one of the ponies had been injured. They'd all be in their beds now, fast asleep. But the Rawling family wasn't sleeping. Instead, they were standing in the dimly lit veterinary clinic, waiting for Star to wake up enough so she could climb back into the horse trailer and go home.

Doesn't Anyone Care?

The grass was still damp with dew as Kendra hurried outside early the next morning. Zipper nickered as Kendra walked in his direction. *"Food,"* he seemed to be saying. *"Where's the food?"*

For once Kendra didn't stop to visit the other ponies. She crawled through the metal bars of the small pen that her father had set up for Star the night before.

"Maybe," Kendra said softly. Maybe it had been a bad dream. Maybe in the dark the injury had seemed worse than it really was. Maybe—just maybe—Star would be healthy enough to ride that day.

"Come here, Star," Kendra called. The little mare lifted her head and blinked her gentle brown eyes.

The pony still looked beautiful from this side.

Kendra's heart lifted for a moment. Then Star took a stiff step forward, and Kendra was able to see the opposite shoulder.

The white pony's silky chest was covered by a stain of dried blood. Even her left leg had streaks of red where the blood had dripped downward. And Star was limping worse that morning. She seemed sore and awkward as she walked a few steps across the tiny pen.

Kendra sighed sadly.

She had thought—she had hoped—that Star was going to be OK. But she wasn't.

Kendra climbed back over the fence and threw a sweet-smelling flake of hay into Star's little pen. Blondie and Zipper whinnied from their side of the corral, so the girl took a moment and fed them some hay. Then she refilled Star's water bucket.

"We won't be going to the gymkhana," Kendra told the pony. She reached inside and gently stroked Star's soft forehead. "My little Starless Star."

Years earlier, Kendra's older sister had owned the pony. Back then, Star had been a deep gray color. And on her dished forehead there had been a perfect white star. That was why she came up with the pony's registered name—A Perfect Star.

As Star got older, she had become lighter and lighter in color. Now she was pure white, and the star was no longer visible.

There were many things about the pony that other people didn't know. Kendra knew everything about her, because Star was her special friend. In fact, in many ways, Star was Kendra's best friend.

How could she leave her best friend behind that day? Megan and Ruth-Ann would want Kendra to come to the gymkhana with them. They could use an extra hand to take care of their ponies, and it would be fun to watch the games. Kendra had thought about it all night, wondering what she should do. Should she stay home with Star? Or go to the Alliance Sports Day with the Ready to Ride Club?

Kendra stood still and thought some more. She still didn't know what to do.

While Kendra was thinking, Mrs. Lewis's brown car drove into the yard. Megan and Ruth-Ann tumbled out of the vehicle, calling "Goodbye" and "See you later" as Mrs. Lewis drove away.

"Guess what I brought for the ponies?" Ruth-Ann asked, bouncing toward Kendra. "Jelly beans for Zipper and a banana for Blondie. And alfalfa cubes for Star, since she doesn't eat anything silly."

"Star's a serious pony," Megan said. "She isn't goofy like the others."

"Star isn't coming today," Kendra said. She bit her lip, determined not to cry.

"What?" Both girls stared at her.

"Not coming?" Ruth-Ann asked. "Why not?"

"Are you sick?" Megan asked.

"You look awful," Ruth-Ann decided.

"I bet you've got the flu," Megan said.

"My little brother Mikey had the flu last week," Ruth-Ann said. "He threw up all over the kitchen floor. Wouldn't it be awful if you threw up when you were riding your pony?"

"Yuck!" Megan said. "That would be so embarrassing!"

"I'm not sick," Kendra said. "Star was hurt last night."

Kendra told them about the evening fireworks and how the ponies had galloped panic-stricken around the corral. "Star ran into the fence and ripped her shoulder open really, really deep," Kendra finished. "We had to take her to the vet in the middle of the night. I would have phoned you, but my parents said it was too late when we got home."

"What about Blondie?" Megan asked, looking anxiously over the fence. "Did she get hurt too?"

"Or Zipper?" Ruth-Ann asked. "Is he injured?"

"They're both OK," Kendra said. "Blondie has a small scrape on her face, and Zipper doesn't have a mark on him."

"Blondie hurt her face?" Megan exclaimed. "Let me see!" She scrambled over the wooden fence and peered carefully at the Palomino mare.

Blondie snuffled and sniffed her master cheerfully. Zipper ambled over, flicking his penny-colored ears. *"Got any food to eat?"* he seemed to ask.

"Blondie's fine," Kendra said. "But look at poor Star!"

Megan didn't look up. Instead, she carefully circled Blondie, checking both sides of the mare's amber face. "The scrape's awfully deep," she finally announced. She pushed Blondie's creamy forelock out of the way. "And it's in a bad location. Her bridle is going to rub right against the sore spot."

"It's just a little scratch," Kendra said.

"Maybe Blondie should have gone to the veterinarian too," Megan said.

"My mom said it was OK," Kendra said.

"But your mom isn't a vet," Megan argued.

"She knows a lot about horses," Kendra said.

"Maybe it seems like a tiny scratch to you," Megan said. "But Blondie's my horse and I'm worried about her. You should have phoned us."

"It didn't even bleed," Kendra said. This time her voice was a bit sharper. Megan didn't seem interested in Star's injury.

"I thought your family was going to take good care of my horse," Megan continued on. "And then this happens."

"It certainly wasn't our fault," Kendra said. "We didn't even know the neighbors were going to shoot off fireworks!" Kendra felt her stomach tighten as she said the words. Could the accident have been partially her fault? What would have happened if she had thought of the ponies sooner? Maybe she could have stopped the fireworks and things would have turned out different."

"I wonder if I should skip the Alliance gymkhana," Megan said. "I think I should phone my mom. She should have a good look at Blondie's face. We might need to go to the vet clinic instead of the sports day."

"I'm sorry, Megan," Kendra said softly.

Megan didn't look up from her pony. "Poor Blondie," she said.

"I'm sure she's going to be OK," Kendra said. "But look at Star. Her shoulder's awful."

"I bet Blondie's going to end up with a scar on her forehead," Megan said.

"It isn't a deep cut," Kendra said.

"I scraped my knee last summer and now I have a mark there," Megan said. "It wasn't deep, either."

"But—"

"My mom and dad are going to be really mad," Megan continued.

Kendra felt a white-hot flash of anger dissolve her

lingering feelings of guilt. She jerked her head up and glared at Megan. "Blondie is totally fine!" Kendra shouted. "She has a tiny bit of hair rubbed off her face. It's Star that you should be worrying about—not your stupid pony!"

"Blondie isn't stupid," Megan said. She thrust her hands on her hips and glared back at Kendra.

"Maybe Blondie isn't stupid," Kendra said. "But you sure are!"

An expression of surprise and hurt flashed across Megan's face. She opened her mouth, but nothing came out.

There was quiet for a moment. Even the three ponies stopped swishing their tails and stood silent, as though they realized something was wrong.

Finally, Ruth-Ann spoke. "Please don't fight," she said. Her face flushed beet red under her short black hair.

"My pony has been seriously hurt, and all anyone can think about is Blondie's tiny little scrape!" Kendra yelled. "Don't you even care about us?"

"I care—" Megan started to say.

"I'm not coming to the gymkhana today," Kendra said, interrupting. "You can tell your parents anything you want. So what if you're all mad at me? I'm going to stay home with Star. She's my best friend. And we don't want to be in the Ready to Ride Club anymore!"

SUPER STAR PROBLEMS

Without giving her friends a chance to reply, Kendra spun around and raced off to the house.

As she ran, Kendra could hear her parents calling out something in the distance, but she didn't wait to hear what they were saying. Instead, she rushed into the house, down the hallway, and into the bathroom. It was the only room with a lock. Kendra made certain she bolted the door firmly before sitting down with a thud on the lid of the toilet.

Hot tears streaked down Kendra's face and fell onto her T-shirt.

They had worked for weeks to prepare for the gymkhana races. Star was a wonderful games pony. Kendra had been certain that they were going to win ribbons that day—maybe even a lot of ribbons.

Perhaps Star and Kendra would have been the high point team in the youth category. Kendra hadn't said anything about that prize out loud, but she certainly had thought about it. The youth pair with the most points always won a big golden trophy.

Kendra had cleared a place on her bedroom dresser to set the trophy. But now someone else would take the prize home. Someone else would win the ribbons and prizes.

Kendra and Star weren't even going to enter the games. And the Ready to Ride Club didn't seem to care.

The Alliance Sports Day

Before long, there was a knock on the bathroom door. Kendra sniffed loudly and didn't answer, but the knock came again. "Kendra, open the door," Mrs. Rawling called.

"I don't want to."

"Open the door," Mrs. Rawling ordered firmly.

Kendra rolled her eyes and unlocked the bathroom door.

"Get your riding boots," Mrs. Rawling said. "And don't forget your lunch. Your dad and the other girls have gone ahead of us with the truck and trailer."

"I'm not going to the gymkhana," Kendra said.

"Yes, you are," Mrs. Rawling said.

"But Star—"

"I'm quite aware Star won't be going," Mrs.

53

Rawling said. "And I know that you're upset about a lot of things right now. But you can't stay home by yourself, and I've already told the Lewis and Chow families that I would be there today to help their girls. They need me. We have to go."

"I'll be OK at home alone," Kendra said.

"I'm not going to leave a ten-year-old home alone all day," Mrs. Rawling said.

"I'm almost eleven," Kendra replied.

"I'm not leaving an almost-eleven-year-old alone at home, either," Mrs. Rawling said. "Hurry, the gymkhana starts in just over an hour."

"But I'm mad at Megan," Kendra said. "I am *not* going to help her."

Mrs. Rawling sighed. "Listen, Kendra," she said a bit impatiently, "I know that you and Megan had an argument. You can tell me all about it in the car on the way to Alliance. I also know that you're upset because Star's injured, and you can't ride in the games." Her mother's face softened. "I don't blame you for being upset. But even if we are upset, we still have responsibilities." Mrs. Rawling hurried out the bathroom door.

Kendra slowly picked up her brush and ran it through her long brown hair before heading toward the kitchen to pick up her lunch.

Kendra's parents could force her go to the Alliance Sports Day. They could force her do a lot of things. But they could not force her to be friends with Megan and Ruth-Ann.

Maybe Blondie and Zipper would misbehave. Maybe Blondie would buck and Megan would fall off. Maybe Zipper would trip and fall over. Maybe Megan and Ruth-Ann wouldn't be able to race their ponies. Then they'd know how it felt for Kendra.

It would serve them right, Kendra thought.

In the car, she turned her face to the window and didn't talk to her mother any more than absolutely necessary for the entire trip to town.

The fairgrounds were bustling with crowds of people talking and laughing. Horses stood tied to nearby horse trailers, some pawing impatiently and others contentedly munching on hay. In the distance, music came from a small merry-go-round and kiddy car ride.

Mrs. Rawling saw where her husband had parked their truck and trailer and parked close by. Kendra saw that Blondie and Zipper stood tied to the trailer. Megan and Ruth-Ann were near them, already dressed in their best riding clothes. They were wearing long-sleeved Western shirts and new blue jeans with shiny belt buckles.

Mrs. Rawling got out of the car, but Kendra stayed inside and watched. The other two girls were scurrying around, picking out the ponies' hooves and preparing to saddle Zipper and Blondie.

Zipper let out a huge sneeze as Ruth-Ann stood directly in front of him holding the bridle. *Good,* Kendra thought. Maybe Ruth-Ann's yellow shirt would have disgusting splashes of horse spit on it now. But Ruth-Ann didn't seem worried; instead, she grinned at the little horse as though Zipper was playing a silly joke.

And maybe he was.

Kendra knew that the girls would want to warm up their ponies before the gymkhana officially began. In the riding ring were a dozen or more horses trotting around, bending and flexing their muscles.

Normally, Kendra would be rushing too, getting Star prepared for the day. Now she had nothing important to do. Star was at home, locked in her little pen, and Kendra was so angry at her Ready to Ride friends that she didn't feel like watching the races.

It was going to be a totally rotten day, Kendra decided, and it wasn't even nine in the morning yet!

Mr. Rawling came over to the car and knocked on the window. Kendra rolled the window down. "Hi," he said.

"Hi," Kendra answered back glumly.

"Did you see Zipper's big sneeze?" he asked.

Kendra nodded her head.

"What did the sick pony say to the doctor?" Mr. Rawling asked.

"Dad, Zipper isn't sick," Kendra said. "And I don't feel like riddles today."

Mr. Rawling didn't seem to hear. "The pony said, 'Doctor, I feel a little hoarse.' "

Kendra rolled her eyes.

"Get it?" Mr. Rawling said. "A pony is a little horse, right?"

"I get it, Dad,"

"What has four legs and flies?" Mr. Rawling went on.

"An ugly bird," Kendra said.

"When did you ever see a bird with four legs?" Mr. Rawling asked.

"Never," Kendra said. "But I know the answer is a horse because horses have flies. I've heard the same jokes a million times before, Dad."

"You have?"

"Yes, Daddy," Kendra said. "You tell the same horse jokes to the Ready to Ride Club every time you see us."

"Really?" Mr. Rawling asked. "What about the joke about the small white horse and the tall black horse?"

"I've heard it."

"What about the one about the three-legged horse

and the pirate?" Mr. Rawling asked thoughtfully.

Kendra hesitated. "Hmm," she said. "I don't think I've heard that one before."

"Me neither," Mr. Rawling said with a grin. "I was just checking to see if you were paying attention."

"Dad!"

"Come out of the car, Kendra," Mr. Rawling said. "I know you've had a bad morning, but your friends need our help. You and I could haul water and hang up the hay bags while they're warming up their ponies."

"They aren't my friends anymore," Kendra said. "And I don't feel like helping them."

Mr. Rawling reached over and opened the car door. He stood back and motioned for Kendra to get out.

With a frown Kendra climbed out of the car. She folded her hands across her chest as she walked toward the horse trailer. *I'm not going to talk to Megan and Ruth-Ann,* she thought. *Especially to Megan.*

Megan should say she's sorry, Kendra continued in her angry thoughts. *If she's really, really sorry, I guess I'll talk to her. But I bet she doesn't say she's sorry. I bet she's glad that Star got hurt and isn't here. That way she can win all the games today instead of Star and me.*

A Motorcycle Scare

The horse trailer was deserted by the time Kendra got there. In the distance, she saw Ruth-Ann and Megan on their ponies in the warm-up ring. They were trotting around in big circles, carefully weaving in and out of the other horses and riders.

"I'll go register the girls at the office," Mr. Rawling said. "Can you get a pail or two of water?"

Kendra sighed. She was dressed in her best riding clothes, and she didn't have a horse of her own to ride. Looking down at her new blue shirt, she frowned. She had bought it with money earned from babysitting. It was never too much work to take care of Star at a horse show. But that day, chores like hauling water suddenly seemed like a real nuisance.

It would be better to get the jobs done quickly, she

decided, before the other girls returned to the trailer. *Then I can go back and sit in the car,* Kendra thought glumly. She wished she had brought a book to read. She had never been bored at a horse event before.

Kendra picked up a purple water bucket and trudged over to the water tap. An older woman wearing an oversized straw cowboy hat was ahead of her, filling several buckets with water. She turned and smiled at Kendra. "It's going to be a real humdinger of a day today, isn't it?" the woman asked.

"A humdinger?"

"A scorcher," the woman continued. "It's going to be hot enough to fry an egg on a sidewalk today. If we had a sidewalk, that is."

"Well, it is a bit warm already," Kendra replied, feeling the sun on the back of her neck.

"Warm?" the woman said. "Why, we're going to roast alive. Good thing I got my ten-gallon hat to keep my head cool."

"Uh-huh," Kendra said and nodded.

"Where's your hat?" the woman asked. "Aren't you riding today?"

"Not today," Kendra replied.

"Not riding?" the woman asked. "I've seen you around before, on a little white pony, right?"

"That's my pony, Star," Kendra said.

"And you aren't riding him today?"

"Star's a girl," Kendra said. "She's at home today." Kendra didn't intend to explain the entire problem to a complete stranger.

The woman's pails were finally full. "Looks like I'm done like dinner," she said, passing the hose to Kendra. Then she lifted her head and tipped her hat back. "Good gravy!" the woman exclaimed. "Look! What in tarnation is coming our way?"

A group of noisy dirt bikes swarmed down the road by the outdoor riding ring. The bike riders wore brightly colored racing helmets, and Kendra couldn't clearly see any of their faces. But she was almost positive one of the riders was her neighbor, Matthew Van Dresser!

"Don't those boys realize they're going to scare the horses?" the woman asked with a frown. The motorcycles howled and roared loud enough to almost cover the woman's words.

Kendra spoke loudly. "I don't think Zipper and Blondie—"

The motorcycles were directly across from the riding ring when there was a sudden loud *bang!* as one of the bikes backfired. Kendra flinched and dropped the purple bucket.

"Jumpin' Jehoshaphat!" the woman in the cowboy hat exclaimed. "Somebody's about to bite the dirt!"

Several horses that were tied nearby spooked at the sound. In the riding ring, a flurry of movement began as horses scattered in different directions.

Kendra tried to spot Megan and Ruth-Ann. Were they OK? Surely Blondie and Zipper would be sensible, even with the loud noise.

Kendra finally spotted Blondie's distinct pale color. She was trotting toward the exit of the ring, her ears pinned against her head. Suddenly, a bay horse in the crowd sprang sideways and, as Kendra watched, crashed directly into Blondie!

"Ride 'em, cowboy!" the woman yelled.

"Megan!" Kendra shouted and rushed toward the riding ring.

With a final roar, the motorcycles disappeared down the road as quickly as they had appeared.

Ruth-Ann, still riding Zipper, met Kendra at the gate of the riding ring. "Zipper's OK," Ruth-Ann said. "But I'm kinda scared. Some of the other horses are freaking out!" She hurried past Kendra and headed toward the horse trailer.

Kendra looked around, trying to locate Blondie. The horses in the riding ring had stopped being spooked. Several mothers were in the arena, helping the smaller riders dismount. Older riders had pulled their horses back to a walk.

Finally, Blondie appeared, but Megan wasn't riding her. Instead, she walked behind the pony as Mrs. Rawling held a firm grip on the reins. Blondie's head was high in the air, and her eyes were wide and frightened. She skittered to the right, and Mrs. Rawling had to pull her straight. Then the pony spooked in the other direction with a loud snort.

When Megan saw Kendra she called out, "I didn't fall off, honest."

Blondie snorted again and danced around, almost stepping on Mrs. Rawling's toes. "Smarten up!" Kendra's mother said, jerking on the reins. She managed to lead Blondie out of the ring, but the pony pranced sideways instead of following properly.

"I vaulted off Blondie as soon as the other horse ran into us," Megan continued. "I landed on my feet, and I'm fine."

"I've never seen your pony behave like this before," Mrs. Rawling said.

"Blondie doesn't mean to be bad," Megan said. "She was scared by the motorcycles, especially when that one made the big bang. But she was still listening to me until that horse crashed into us!"

"Don't forget she had that big scare last night," Mrs. Rawling said. "That probably is making things even worse." Blondie circled Mrs. Rawling and then tossed her head in the air. "Whoa!" Mrs. Rawling ordered.

Blondie came to a halt for a moment and then pawed the ground impatiently with her small black hoof.

"Ruth-Ann," Mrs. Rawling called. "Could you bring Zipper over here? Maybe Blondie will calm down when she has her friend nearby."

Ruth-Ann rode the little sorrel Paint up to Blondie. Zipper nudged the mare with his muzzle, but Blondie didn't pay any attention. Instead, she snorted and shook her head harder. Her thick blond mane flapped back and forth.

"I can hold her, Mrs. Rawling," Megan said. "I think she'll listen to me."

Mrs. Rawling looked doubtful, but she passed the reins to the girl.

"It's OK, Blondie," Megan crooned to the pony. "I'm here to take care of you. Those motorcycles are gone now."

The loudspeaker suddenly crackled in the distance. "The show will start in five minutes," a voice announced. "The first class will be ten and under barrel racing."

Blondie narrowed her eyes and pinned her ears. The loudspeaker popped again and Blondie jumped forward.

"Whoa," Megan ordered. She pulled back as hard as she could.

Blondie snorted and reared up on her back legs.

Megan let go of the reins with a squeal and jumped backwards. Mrs. Rawling managed to catch the reins before the pony stepped on them. She made the pony circle around her twice and then tried to pull her to a stop.

"I quit!" Megan said nervously. "I'm supposed to be in the fifth class with Ruth-Ann. But how can I ride if Blondie's behaving like this?"

"I don't know," Mrs. Rawling said. She looked worried. "I wonder what your mom would do with Blondie."

"I could phone her at work," Megan said.

"Well, let's see what we can do first," Mrs. Rawling said. "Let's halter Blondie and tie her to the horse trailer for a while. Maybe she'll calm down once she realizes she isn't going anywhere."

It was difficult for Mrs. Rawling to steady Blondie long enough to slip off the bridle and put on the halter, but she managed. Then she tied Blondie to the horse trailer and stepped back.

"Maybe I won't need to use the truck this afternoon," Mr. Rawling said, walking over to the group.

"Why won't you need the truck?" Mrs. Rawling asked.

"The way Blondie's behaving, it looks as though

she'll pull the trailer home by herself," Mr. Rawling said. "That will save us a few dollars in gas, won't it?"

"I don't think this is the time or place to joke around, Rob," Mrs. Rawling said. "Megan could have been hurt."

"Horses are dangerous," Mr. Rawling said. "That's why I want you girls to take up something safe, like knitting."

"Robert," Mrs. Rawling warned.

"They could be the R2K Club," Mr. Rawling continued. "Ready to Knit."

"Make yourself useful," Mrs. Rawling said, "and pass us the hay bags. Maybe Blondie will relax if she has something to distract her."

Kendra quickly passed the loaded net to her mother.

Blondie wouldn't touch the hay. Instead, she walked forward as far as her lead rope would allow, and then wiggled around to the left and then the right. When she couldn't go any farther, she began to paw again.

"She's acting like a monster," Megan said. "I'll never be able to handle her when she's like this." Megan looked as though she was about to cry as she watched her pony fuss at the end of the lead rope.

Mr. Rawling stopped joking when he saw how upset the girl was. He put his arm around her and gave her a squeeze before offering to go over to the office and explain that Megan wouldn't be showing in the first few classes.

"I've never seen Blondie act like this before," Ruth-Ann said. "She wasn't this bad even at the Hardisty Cancer Trail Ride."

"She's really scared," Megan said. "And now she won't listen to me."

Kendra stood off to the side, quietly watching. A short time before, she had been hoping that Megan would have problems with Blondie. Now it was really happening. But Kendra didn't feel as happy as she had expected. Instead, she felt a bit sorry for Megan. It wasn't any fun having a pony and not being able to ride.

Trish Solves the Problem

The barrel races were going to take a long time as there were a number of classes for the different age groups of children, and then the adults. Mrs. Rawling suggested the girls leave Blondie and Zipper saddled and tied to the trailer while they waited.

"Maybe Blondie will settle down if we leave her alone," she suggested. So the three girls walked over to the wooden grandstands to watch.

No one seemed sure who to sit by. Finally, Megan and Ruth-Ann sat side by side in the first row. Kendra sat directly behind them.

The thirteen and under barrel racing class was about to begin—the class Kendra and Star would have entered if Star had not been injured. Kendra watched each of the horses and ponies with great interest. Some of the horses behaved horribly, rushing past the barrels and not turning at the proper time. Some of the riders turned neatly around the barrels but stayed at a steady trot instead of cantering. A few pairs had obviously practiced more, and they galloped around the barrels properly.

"Star would have run faster than any of them," Ruth-Ann commented when the race was finished. "You and Super Star would have easily won the class, Kendra."

Kendra nodded her head and watched as the girl with the fastest time picked up a big red rosette.

Before long, it was time for Ruth-Ann and Megan's first event—the egg and spoon race. They headed over to the trailer to collect their ponies. Zipper cooperated as Ruth-Ann quickly bridled him and then mounted. She rode off to wait for her turn in the ring. Blondie had not settled down while the girls were away. She continued to paw and fidget while tied to the horse trailer. Anxiously she tossed her head every time Megan tried to touch her.

"She's still jumpy," Megan said. "How can I balance a hard-boiled egg on a spoon if she's spooking around the place?"

"I don't trust Blondie right now," Mrs. Rawling said. "She's still so upset, she isn't even thinking."

"Do you think she'd be OK if I put her to work?" Megan asked.

Mrs. Rawling shook her head. "Someone could get hurt," she said.

"What am I supposed to do?" Megan asked, her forehead wrinkling under her riding helmet.

"I don't know," Mrs. Rawling said. "Maybe I should phone your mother."

"That might be a good idea," Megan said. She reached over and tried to pat the Palomino pony, but Blondie jerked her head up and stamped her hoof impatiently. Megan pulled her foot out of the way just in time and frowned at her pony.

Mrs. Rawling gave the pony one last glance and walked away, opening her cell phone as she went.

Megan looked at Kendra. Kendra looked back at her. Neither of them smiled. Finally, Megan spoke. "What should I do?"

Kendra shrugged. "I don't know."

Kendra turned around and saw Ruth-Ann guiding Zipper into the ring for their class. Adults on foot handed a spoon and an egg to each of the riders. This would be a fairly easy class for Ruth-Ann, since Zipper had a smooth jog and lope. Kendra wanted to watch, but then something caught her eye. Near the grandstands stood a tall woman with blond hair pulled back in a ponytail.

"Look!" Kendra said. "It's Trish!" Trish Klein was the girls' riding instructor. She had helped the girls prepare for the day's gymkhana races, but they hadn't expected to see her at the events.

Both girls waved their hands and called to her.

Trish smiled and waved at the girls. "Hi!" she called, and she walked in their direction. "I thought I'd come watch the Ready to Ride Club for a while," she said. Then she stopped and stared at the Palomino pony, who continued to fuss by the trailer. "Wow!" she said. "What's wrong with Blondie?"

The entire story took a few minutes to tell, starting with the fireworks at the Rawlings' house and Star's injury and ending with Blondie's motorcycle scare and the horse crash.

Trish listened carefully. "You girls certainly have quite the adventures," she said when the story was finished.

"What should we do?" Megan asked. "We've practiced so much at home. And I really want to ride today."

"I did too," Kendra said.

"Well, of course you did," Trish said. "But there are no guarantees in life, especially if you own horses!"

"But—" Megan began.

"But nothing," Trish said. "We can try a few things to help Blondie relax and focus on you. If she settles down, you might be able to ride. But we cannot force Blondie's brain to think a certain way. And she must be paying attention to you before you can show her."

"So I should just give up?" Megan asked.

"No," Trish said. "We aren't going to give up yet. But just be aware that even if Blondie does relax, she might not be safe to show today."

"Mom went to phone Mrs. Lewis," Kendra said. "Maybe she'll have an idea what we should do."

"Well, until then, I have a suggestion," Trish said.

"What?"

"Did you girls bring the longe line?" Trish asked.

"I never longe Blondie," Megan said.

"Did you bring it?" Trish repeated.

Kendra nodded her head and walked to the back of the truck. Picking up the longe line from the truck bed, she brought it to Trish.

"Good," Trish said. "We need to get Blondie to focus on us. The best way to do that is to longe her." Trish expertly slid Blondie's bridle back onto the restless pony and then snapped the longe line onto the snaffle bit. "That will give us more control than usual," the woman said.

She picked up the longe line and clicked her tongue.

"Are you allowed to work with horses now?" Kendra asked worriedly. Trish had been diagnosed with breast cancer several months earlier and had surgery to remove the cancerous lump. The doctor had instructed her to avoid anything that would cause strain.

"Don't worry," Trish said. "I won't overdo it." She led Blondie forward to an open patch of grass. In a moment, Blondie was trotting and then galloping around her. The pony's body showed worry as she moved with her head straight up in the air and her tail up, as though she was a little Arabian instead of a half-Welsh and half-Morgan pony.

Trish held on to the lead rope firmly as the pony jerked and pulled. She made the mare canter around her for a few minutes, and then reversed her to move the other direction. Blondie snorted and spun around, throwing up pieces of sod with her hooves.

"It's not enough that we get Blondie physically tired," Trish explained as she held the longe line firmly. "I also need to find a way to get her thinking instead of just reacting. So changing directions frequently is important."

For the next few minutes, Blondie cantered and then Trish stopped her and turned her the opposite direction, sending her into a canter again. Before long, Blondie began to huff and slow down.

Trish continued to patiently direct the mare. She

didn't argue with Blondie when she wanted to rush, but just kept her moving in the right direction.

"The worst thing you can do with a spooked horse is to try and force them to stand still," Trish said finally. "Sometimes they need action and movement to feel safe. But we have to make sure her actions aren't going to hurt us or anyone else."

Blondie broke into a trot and circled twice at that speed before rushing off at a canter again. "She's starting to look tired," Kendra said.

"Good," Trish said. She let out the longe line so Blondie's circle was slightly larger and encouraged the pony to keep moving.

Blondie circled several more times and then broke back into a trot again. This time, the little mare stayed at a fast trot. Her head was still held high, but now her tail was more relaxed.

"Turn," Trish ordered. She raised her whip and forced the mare to change directions. Blondie spun around and trotted off again.

"She's getting calmer," Kendra said.

"If Blondie starts paying more attention to me, then she'll also start paying less attention to the frightening things around her," Trish said. "It's almost impossible to think about two things at once. I want her to think about us and not to think about being scared."

Blondie finally let out a sigh and broke into a walk for a few strides before trotting off again. But now her trot was slower, and her head was much more relaxed.

"Good girl!" Megan said. Blondie flicked her ears at the girl.

"People are the same way," Trish said. She shifted the longe line to her other hand and asked Blondie to change directions before continuing to speak. "Sometimes we get really focused on all the bad things around us, and we forget to focus on God. And then God can't help us very easily."

"I'm like that sometimes," Kendra said. Suddenly, she felt ashamed of how angry she had been at Megan and Ruth-Ann that morning. She had been so busy getting mad at her friends that she hadn't even taken a moment to ask God to help her!

"We're all like that sometimes," Trish agreed. "Even grown-ups get too busy. God has to find ways to direct us so that we start paying attention to Him instead of all the other junk around us. And when we pay attention to God, He can use us in the best possible ways. When we focus on stuff around us, instead of God, then we aren't much use to anyone."

Blondie was walking now. Her ears continued to swivel back and forth.

Finally, Trish beckoned to the girls. "Here, Megan,"

she called. "It's time you longed your pony yourself."

"Do you think she'll be OK?" Megan asked.

Trish nodded her head. "I'll stay nearby," she said. "But my arm is really starting to hurt."

Megan quickly took the longe line and clicked her tongue to start Blondie back into a steady trot.

Trish walked away to the side and then motioned for Kendra. "Having a bad day, Kenny girl?" she asked.

"Awful," Kendra said.

"It's a big worry when someone you love gets hurt, isn't it," Trish commented.

"Yes," Kendra said. "And I really wanted to compete in the games today. I thought we'd do really well."

"Why are you angry at Megan?" Trish asked.

Kendra was startled. They had told Trish all about the ponies, but neither of the girls had mentioned anything about the fight that morning. "What makes you think I'm mad at anyone?" she asked.

"Kendra," Trish said. Her voice was soft and warm.

Kendra looked at Trish and felt tears fill her eyes. She began to explain what had happened. "I thought Megan and Ruth-Ann were my friends," she said. "And all they could think about was Blondie. They didn't even care about Star and me."

"Megan and Ruth-Ann love Star," Trish said.

"And they love you too. But Megan was obviously really upset. She cares about Blondie so much that she overreacted. And it sounds as though Ruth-Ann didn't know what to do, so she didn't do anything."

"I don't know if they should be my friends anymore," Kendra said.

Trish looked Kendra straight in the eye. "I thought we had this talk before," the woman said.

"We've never talked about the Ready to Ride Club fighting before," Kendra said. "Because we've never argued before."

"Yes," Trish said. "But last year you had a lot of problems when you tried to teach Star how to jump. Do you remember what I told you when you were frustrated with your pony?"

"What?"

"I told you that Star was a good pony, but she wasn't perfect," Trish said. "Even if her real name is A Perfect Star! Remember?"

Kendra nodded her head.

"Only God is perfect," Trish said. "Your pony is a good pony, but she still does things wrong sometimes. And no person is perfect either. That's why we all need Jesus to pay the price for sin. We all make mistakes. But He can forgive us and help us to be better."

"I know," Kendra said quietly.

"If you had friends who always acted badly, then I would suggest that you consider finding different friends," Trish said. "But Megan and Ruth-Ann do not act badly all the time. In fact, they're special people. They just aren't perfect people. They acted wrong today, and it sounds like you did too, in return."

"I guess," Kendra said.

"I want you to have a serious talk with Megan when she's finished working with Blondie," Trish said. "It's OK to explain why you're upset. Talking about problems is the best way to solve them."

Megan brought Blondie to a halt in front of Kendra and Trish. "She's listening to me," the girl said. "Look." She walked over to Blondie and tugged on the longe line. Blondie hesitated and then backed up a step.

"Good girl," Trish said. "Now, take her back to the trailer and see if she'll have something to eat."

"OK."

When Blondie and Megan had disappeared around the trailer, Kendra turned back to Trish. "Do I have to talk to Megan about our problem?" she asked. "It's kinda embarrassing."

"Yes," Trish said. "You do. Problems aren't solved unless you actively do something about them."

"But—"

"Kendra," Trish said. "I want to help you. But

you need to decide if you're going to trust God or not."

"I trust God," Kendra said.

"Then follow His advice," Trish said. "If we have problems with someone, the Bible says we are supposed to go to that person and talk about it. That's what I want you to do."

Kendra nodded her head slowly.

Kendra trusted Trish, because she had helped her many times in the past. And she also trusted God. So if Trish and God wanted something from her, then she would try to do it.

Even if it would be difficult.

A Talk With Megan

"I'm sorry," Megan said. She had been brushing Blondie while they talked, but now she put the curry-comb down. "I really am sorry, and I've wanted to tell you that all morning."

Kendra was so startled at Megan's admission, she almost dropped the full water bucket. "Why didn't you just say that?" she finally asked.

"I didn't think you'd listen," Megan said. "You were really mad at me!"

Kendra nodded her head. "I know," she said. "And I was wrong to be so grumpy. I'm sorry too."

"It's OK," Megan said.

The girls shyly smiled at each other. Blondie swished her tail at a horsefly, almost swatting Megan in the arm, and then took a big bite of hay from the bag.

A Talk With Megan

Trish appeared in a moment. "It looks as though things are getting back to normal," she said.

"I'm not mad at Megan anymore," Kendra said.

Trish laughed. "I meant Blondie!" she said. "Not you girls!"

"Can I ride Blondie today?" Megan asked. "We've only missed a couple of our classes."

"What classes are next?" Trish asked.

"The boot race," Megan said. "And the sack race and something called the surprise race, whatever that is."

"Megan," Trish said. "I know you don't want to hear this, but I honestly don't think you should show Blondie today. She's calmed down now, and is much more relaxed. But think how the boot race works."

"It's fun!" Kendra said. "Everyone puts their boots in a pile and then you ride down as fast as you can and find your boots!"

"That's right," Trish said. "And what is Blondie going to do when you race her down to the end and other horses crowd around her?"

"Oh," Megan said. "She'd probably freak out again!"

"Probably," Trish said. "I would suggest you ride her around here, but keep away from the other horses. There will always be other days to ride in gymkhanas."

A voice called loudly from the other side of the

horse trailer. "I need to borrow someone's boots!" Ruth-Ann called.

The girls walked around the trailer to see what Ruth-Ann was talking about.

"My Roper boots lace up," Ruth-Ann said. "They'll be much too hard to get on and off in a hurry during the boot race. Can I borrow yours, Kendra? You won't be riding, will you?"

"Of course, you can use my boots," Kendra said.

"No," Megan said. "Don't use hers. Use mine."

Ruth-Ann's face suddenly looked worried. "You guys aren't still fighting, are you?" she asked.

"We aren't fighting," Kendra said. "The Ready to Ride Club never fights."

"Sometimes they do," Trish said with a smile. "But they're smart enough to work their way through problems."

"But you should use my boots, because they're special," Megan said. She yanked off one boot and held it up. "Look!"

The bottom half of Megan's boots were made of shiny black leather, but the top portion was a brilliant pink color. "They'll be perfect in the boot race!" Megan said. "You'll easily see which ones to get."

With a laugh, the two girls swapped boots, and then Kendra and Megan hurried Ruth-Ann and Zipper back to the ring.

Ruth-Ann placed third in the boot race, and then won first place in the sack race. She returned to the horse trailer with two ribbons in her hand.

The loudspeaker snapped and popped a few minutes later. "The surprise race will begin in five minutes," the announcer said. "For this race, we will require three people and one horse for each team. It will be perfect for any parents out there who'd like to participate with their child."

Kendra, Megan, and Ruth-Ann looked at each other. "OK, 'Mommy,'" Megan said to Kendra with a grin. "Would you like to try something new?"

Kendra grinned back. "I guess that depends what 'Daddy' has to say!"

"How come I have to be the boy?" Ruth-Ann replied. "Boys are always trouble."

"I heard that," Mr. Rawling said from the far side of the trailer.

"Take your riding helmets," Mrs. Rawling instructed as she approached them.

"I didn't bring my helmet," Kendra said. "I wasn't expecting to ride."

"I have a spare one in my truck," Trish said. "Just a minute."

Soon the Ready to Ride Club and Zipper were in the arena. Five other teams stood nearby.

"This is a relay race," the announcer said. "Except

that instead of using a baton, you use people. Team member one rides the horse first. Team member two stands at one end of the arena, and team member three stands at the other end."

Ruth-Ann stuck her toe in the stirrup and swung onto Zipper's back.

"Team member one must race down to the end of the arena and get off the horse," the announcer continued. "Team member two gets on as quickly as possible and races back to the other end, where they get off, and team member three gets on. The first team that crosses the finish line is the winner."

"We can do that," Megan said.

"Zipper isn't very fast," Ruth-Ann warned. "And you're going to have to really kick him to make him hurry."

"I have an idea that will help us win," Kendra said, speaking quickly as the other teams began to move into place.

"What?"

"We can beat everyone if we get on and off at the same time," Kendra said.

"What do you mean?"

"The person that's riding should get off on Zipper's right side," Kendra said. "The other person could get on at the same time on the left side. That would mean we could exchange people in about half the time the other teams will take."

"Good idea!" Megan said.

"Zipper won't care what side we dismount from," Ruth-Ann said. "He's used to all sorts of things with my brother and sister around."

"Take your places!" the announcer said loudly.

With a final nod to each other, Megan and Kendra hurried to opposite ends of the arena.

When the whistle blew, Zipper came cantering down the arena straight toward Megan. Before Zipper was even totally stopped, Ruth-Ann was sliding out of the saddle on the right side and Megan was clambering up on the other side. With a kick of her heels and a cluck of her tongue, she had Zipper cantering across the ring toward Kendra.

Kendra was prepared. She swung into the saddle as Megan slid off the opposite side. They were in such a hurry that they bumped heads. "Good thing we have our helmets on!" Megan shouted.

Then Kendra was securely in the saddle. She squeezed her legs hard and sent Zipper back toward the finish line. The other two girls hollered encouragement as Zipper streaked across the finish line, far ahead of the other teams.

"R2R rules!" Ruth-Ann shouted. The three girls linked arms and marched across the riding ring to collect their bright first-place ribbons!

Plans for the Next Day

On the way home, the girls talked nonstop. "I didn't know that going to a gymkhana without a horse of my own could be so much fun," Kendra said. Then she reached up and felt her head. "Uh-oh," she groaned. "I forgot to return Trish's riding helmet."

"Maybe we could ask Trish to come over some-time tomorrow and get it," Ruth-Ann suggested. "She could look at Star's sore shoulder."

"Ruth-Ann and I decided we'd come over tomor-row too." Megan said. "We thought we would spend some time with you and Star."

"Star would like the company, I'm sure," Kendra said. "She's going to get really bored locked in that tiny pen for the next few weeks."

"Maybe I should bring Zipper for a visit," Ruth-Ann said.

"And Blondie too," Megan said. "If she's over being a brat."

"She'll be fine tomorrow," Kendra said. "She was back to normal by the end of the gymkhana."

"Ponies aren't ever normal," Mr. Rawling said from the driver's seat. The girls rolled their eyes and ignored the comment.

"We can give Star a beauty makeover," Megan said.

"I'll bring some ribbons for her mane," Ruth-Ann said thoughtfully.

"I'll see if I can borrow my mom's clippers," Megan said. "We could trim her bridle path and all the long hairs on her face."

"She'll look so pretty," Kendra said.

"So the fight's over, is it?" Mr. Rawling asked.

"Fight?" Kendra asked. "We never fight."

"Except with boys," Megan said.

"Boys are yucky," Ruth-Ann agreed. "But the Ready to Ride Club is never yucky."

"I have one more idea," Kendra said. "See if you think I'm crazy."

"You're crazy!" Mr. Rawling said.

"Dad! You haven't even heard my suggestion!"

"I don't have to hear your suggestion," Mr. Rawling

said. "I already know you're crazy."

"I was thinking how bad I felt today, when I was angry at everyone," Kendra said, serious again. "And then I thought how this was all Matt's fault."

"I told you boys are horrid," Ruth-Ann said.

"Well, I don't want to be mad at Matt or his brothers either," Kendra said. "I felt really bad when I was so angry. And God doesn't want us to be mad at others, anyhow."

"Maybe we should find a way to force the Van Dressers to move away!" Megan said. "Then our problems would be over."

"What could we do to get rid of them?" Ruth-Ann wondered.

"How about a tiger?" Mr. Rawling suggested.

"A tiger—Daddy!"

"If we put a tiger in their backyard, it would eat all the boys," Mr. Rawling said. "Then you wouldn't have to worry about them bothering you anymore!"

"That's an excellent idea, Mr. Rawling!" Ruth-Ann agreed.

"But we have to find a tiger," Megan said.

"One that doesn't eat ponies," Mr. Rawling said. "Only boys."

"Daddy, be serious for a minute," Kendra said.

"Tigers are a serious matter," Mr. Rawling said. "Especially if they're trying to eat you."

"I want to invite Matt over tomorrow," Kendra continued.

"I'm pretty certain Matt won't want to do a beauty makeover on Star," Megan said.

"Matt and his family are giving us problems because they don't know anything about ponies," Kendra said. "I think we should invite Matt over and give him some pony lessons."

"Pony lessons?"

"Yeah," Kendra replied. "Maybe Trish could teach Matt to ride. And the Ready to Ride Club could teach him how to take care of ponies. If Matt knew what ponies liked, and what they didn't like, then maybe he wouldn't do anything to scare them."

The girls looked at each other for a moment. "He shouldn't ride Star," Ruth-Ann finally said. "Her shoulder's hurt."

"And she can't exercise for another two weeks," Megan said.

Ruth-Ann sighed. "Matt can ride Zipper," she said. "But only if Trish is there to give him lessons."

"Maybe he'll end up being part of the Ready to Ride Club too," Mr. Rawling said. "Then I could call your club the Ready *Four* Ride Club. Right?"

"Mr. Rawling!"

Kendra's father pulled into the parking lot of a store and parked the truck and horse trailer carefully.

"What are we doing, Dad?" Kendra asked. "Aren't we going to take Blondie and Zipper home?"

"I thought we'd stop for some special congratulations ice-cream cones," Mr. Rawling said.

"Who's buying?" Megan asked.

"Why, I am, of course," Mr. Rawling replied, unfastening his seat belt. "If anyone wants an ice cream, that is."

"I do!" the three girls shrieked together.

"Perfect," Mr. Rawling said. "And I know what flavor we should buy to celebrate your big day, and your plans for tomorrow."

"What flavor, Daddy?" Kendra asked.

"Tiger ice cream, of course," Mr. Rawling said. With a grin he sprang out of the truck and sprinted across the parking lot to the ice-cream store.

The girls jumped out after him.

The day had been a very strange day. It had started with a fight and ended with a fun gymkhana and a plan to solve their next-door-neighbor problem.

Who knew what the next day would bring for the Ready to Ride Club?

Words of Advice on Choosing the Right Pony

My eldest daughter, Danelle, was eleven years old when I set about to buy her the perfect pony. I traveled for many miles, looking at horses that were supposed to be well broken, quiet, sensible, and bombproof. Most of the time, I found horses with obvious problems. One time I drove three hours to see an Arabian-cross mare that was supposed to have been shown by the owner's granddaughter in the past. The horse bucked the first time I got on!

Finally, I found a suitable looking pony. It was a handsome black pony with a thick mane and tail. Casper was a Welsh and Morgan cross and stood about 13.2 hands high, which meant it would be the perfect size for Danelle to handle.

I watched as the teenage owner rode the pony

around the yard. Then I rode the pony. He behaved well as I rode across the countryside, passing obstacles such as spooky mailboxes, fast-moving vehicles, and barking dogs. We trotted and loped happily down shady paths and finally ended the ride crossing a chest-deep stream.

I was certain Casper would be the perfect pony for Danelle. And he was in my price range! So I put money down on Casper that afternoon and picked him up the next day.

Unfortunately, Casper turned out to be less than perfect once we got him home. He had poor ground manners, especially for a child rider, and dragged Danelle from one patch of grass to another. He was completely ring sour, meaning he hated being shown or doing ring work. This made Danelle's first year at 4-H totally miserable, as she was always struggling with the pony while the other children were walking and trotting around the arena.

Trail riding was one thing Casper did well, and in that area Danelle enjoyed the pony. But otherwise, he was a big frustration.

I regretted buying Casper and thought about selling the beast. But by then Danelle had fallen in love with the ornery creature. So she spent the next two years struggling and arguing with a pony that just had to do things his way.

Words of Advice on Choosing the Right Pony

Buying a pony or a horse can be a tough job, even for an experienced rider. I want my books to show that while ponies are wonderful, they do have their bad points! No one should own a horse unless they're prepared for the bad, as well as the good.

Horse riding can be a lot of fun. Your chances for success will increase if

1. you find a quiet, well-trained, and obedient horse or pony;
2. you take lessons or join a riding group, such as 4-H or Pony Club, and have an experienced adult to help you;
3. you are willing to work hard, do lots of ground-work, and ride your horse regularly;
4. you take all the safety precautions possible, such as riding with an approved helmet and high-heeled boots, and ride in a safe environment;
5. you ask God to bless you in your activities, to help you become a kind and knowledgeable horse person, and to help you know what to do when you have problems.

Good luck. I hope you can have the opportunity to enjoy horses as much as I have!

Happy Trails,

Heather Grovet, and her Paint horses, Hailey and Austin, and miniature pony, Taffy

Attention Horse Lovers!

You'll want to read all the books in the Ready to Ride Series.
Ready to Ride Series (Ages 9–12)
Set of books one through three

(Book 1) **A Perfect Star.** Kendra, Ruth-Ann, and Megan form the Ready to Ride (R2R) Club and begin taking riding lessons.

(Book 2) **Zippitty Do Dah.** Ruth-Ann and her friends give pony rides to kids to raise money for an orphanage. They asked God to keep all the riders safe. So why didn't God answer their prayer?

(Book 3) **Good As Gold.** The girls participate in a real horse show, competing against each other. No one could've predicted what would happen and what the girls would learn from it.

Paperbacks.   4333003844. (*Sold in sets only.*)

Blondie's Big Ride   Ready to Ride Series Book #4

It was a hot summer day. The girls and their horses were all tired and uncomfortable. " 'OK, everyone!' called Trish, ... 'Good job! But we need to rest so your ponies don't pass out in this heat.' " None of the girls were prepared for what Trish had to say next.

" 'Girls,' she said slowly, 'I won't be able to teach anyone riding lessons for at least a month. Maybe even longer. . . .

" 'I have some bad news,' Trish said. 'Some very bad news. The doctors say I have cancer.' "

Paperback, 96 pages.   ISBN 13: 978-0-8163-2225-1
ISBN 10: 0-8163-2225-2

A Friend for Zipper   Ready to Ride Series Book #5

What's wrong with this horse? Ruth-Ann's cousin, Kaitlin, bought a pony to train and sell to raise money for her high school tuition. She named him Mystery. Kaitlin worked very hard with her new pony, but instead of becoming more trained, Mystery got worse. Why didn't he respond to her commands?

Ruth-Ann asked her R2R pals to help, and they knew of someone who could give Kaitlin expert advice!

Paperback, 96 pages.   ISBN 13: 978-0-8163-2226-8
ISBN10: 0-8163-2226-0

Order from:
1 Local Adventist Book Center®
2 Call 1-800-765-6955
3 Shop AdventistBookCenter.com.